Get your downloads here

CHARMS
BOOK SERIES

ATTIE'S
AMAZING ADVENTURES

By Loxley Browne

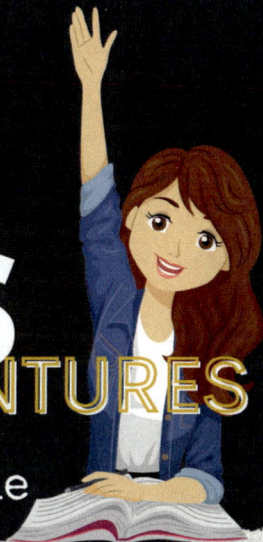

BOOK 1
ROCKET CITY

This book belongs to:

CHARMS Book Series
Attie's Amazing Adventures: Rocket City Love
© 2025 Loxley Browne

Published by Athenian+Browne in the United States of America.
130 Inverness Plaza, Suite 217, Birmingham, Alabama, USA 35242
BeAthenian.org and CharmsBookSeries.com

For information about special discounts for bulk purchases, please contact Athenian+Browne at Charms@BeAthenian.org

Written by Loxley Browne
Cover design and book interior design by Loxley Browne

ISBN: 979-8-9901528-1-6 [Print, Paperback]
ISBN: 979-8-9901528-4-7 [Print, Hardcover]
ISBN: 979-8-9901528-0-9 [eBook]

I hope you enjoy my book and my vision for encouraging girls to explore and dream big at BeAthenian.org. Get your hands dirty!

Loxley

"In every path we choose, there will be obstacles and uncertainties. But remember, it is during these moments of uncertainty that we are given the opportunity to truly grow. Embrace what lies ahead, for even if the road is foggy, your determination will light the way."

Aunt L♡xley

TABLE OF CONTENTS

FOREWARD

It's incredibly important for young girls to feel empowered to explore and discover disparate career paths, knowing with all their hearts that they can truly pursue their passions. Those who are fortunate enough to join Loxley Browne and Athenian get to sample tastes of their future in bite-size pieces, allowing them to see how it feels as they grow.

Over the last four years, I've watched Loxley put her energy into Athenian to helping girls achieve their dreams. She's keen to share her knowledge. She's passionate about tapping into her vast network to give the girls in her fold and beyond what they need to succeed in life. By showing girls they can do "it" – meaning anything – Athenian builds both courage and confidence.

This book series was written to show the world what Athenian stands for and its inspiring messages for girls everywhere.

Give it a read.

Kristin V. Shaw
Automotive Journalist

FOREWARD

It is a privilege to write the forward for a book that not only celebrates this incredible organization but also serves as inspiration for young girls aspiring to make their mark in the fields of STEM, especially in the world of racing and transportation.

My adventure with motorsports began long before Athenian came into my life. The sound of engines, the smell of burning rubber, and the sight of sleek cars racing around the track have always intrigued me. I discovered a world where engineering worked in harmony with strategy. Each race was not just a contest of speed, but teamwork.

There were times when I felt like an outsider, struggling to find my place in this industry, but it was during these moments of doubt that Athenian emerged as a guide.

Athenian, with its unwavering commitment to empowering girls in STEM provided me with a community. Through their programs, I gained not only technical skills but also the confidence to assert myself in a world that often seemed out of reach. Meeting fellow members, mentors, and role models. Each story was unique, yet we shared a common thread—the drive to break barriers and redefine what is possible.

Athenian is not just about creating the next generation of engineers, drivers, and leaders; it's about creating a movement. A movement that encourages girls to dream big, to be bold, and to never shy away from a challenge. This book is a testament to that movement.

As you turn these pages, I invite you to immerse yourself in the world of Athenian. To those considering joining Athenian, I can't wait for you to experience the same sense of wonder and accomplishment that I did.

Let this book be your starting line.

Sachi Goel
Athenian
Former Student Advisory Board President

The amazing adventures I have had with Aunt Loxley have opened my mind to all of the careers that I could pursue to move the world. Now, more than ever, I have to focus and learn key skills that will move me closer to my goal of making a significant impact on the world.

We moved from Creativity Cove, the place where all my previous amazing adventures had taken place. My antics as a five-year old inventor in "Get Your Hands Dirty: The Little Inventor With a Big Dream" ... you should check them out! But now that I have grown up (a bit), my mom decided to start working for a rocket company based in Huntsville, often referred to as the "Rocket City." Huntsville's reputation as a hub for space exploration sealed the deal for my parents, especially considering my dad's IT expertise with the FBI. For them working for companies that both have HQs in the same city would be a first. In Creativity Cove, Dad drove into D.C. and Mom was jetting all over the world. It was natural for us, but calendar management (i.e. project management) is the only thing that kept my parents on track and organized.

I, of course, was thrilled with the idea of a new home and a fresh start. With my sense of adventure and my social butterfly tendencies (thanks to the influence of my incredible Aunt Loxley), I knew this move would open up a world of possibilities. More people to learn from, more stories to hear, and more careers to explore.

Speaking of Aunt Loxley, she has become quite the sensation. Her recent book, "I Can Do It" soared to the top of the NYT bestseller list within days of its release. I couldn't be prouder of her and everything she has accomplished. Her spirit, sense of wonder, and unwavering belief in the power of imagination have always inspired me to keep exploring, creating, and dreaming big.

But let's get back to this recent move. As exciting as it was, nothing worth pursuing comes without a few speed bumps along the way. Moving to a new city meant leaving behind familiar faces and places, exchanging them for the unknown. It meant navigating the complex landscape of a new school, making new friends, and finding my place in this community.

The first few days in our new city were a whirlwind of unpacking, meeting neighbors, and getting acquainted with the lay of the land. Each morning, I woke up to the sound of chirping birds and the fresh scent of grass wafting through my open window. The neighborhood, nestled amidst rolling hills and lush greenery, felt peaceful and inviting. I could sense the friendly nature of the people who lived here, their warmth reaching out to me like an invisible embrace.

As I unpacked my belongings and started organizing my new room, I couldn't help but reflect on the journey that had led me here. From the moment Aunt Loxley introduced me to the wonders of creativity and sparked my passion for invention, I knew I had found my calling. But this move was more than just a change of scenery; it was a chance for me to expand my horizons, learn new things, and discover the vast world of innovation that awaits me.

Attie

CHAPTER 1
The Move and New Beginnings

A lot had happened since the last time anyone read about the "little inventor" in Creativity Cove. The Taylor Swift ERAS tour, the farewell trip with the BFFs to Pittsburgh on June 17, 2023, marked the beginning of an incredible journey for Attie. There were numerous moments during that concert when she and her friends felt as though Taylor was speaking directly to them. It was truly amazing how music had the power to tell a story, especially one that resonated so deeply.

During their trip to Pittsburgh, they had the opportunity to visit Attie's Aunt Loxley, who was working on a mysterious "top secret" project at Carnegie Mellon University. The conversations with Aunt Loxley were filled with mentions of space, gardening, and monarch butterflies, piquing the curiosity of Attie and her friends. Determined to uncover the truth, they made the audacious decision to discreetly follow Aunt Loxley's activities, hoping to catch a glimpse of what she was truly up to.

Clandestine observations led to moments of intrigue. The young inventor spotted Aunt Loxley engaging in hushed conversations with an individual emerging from the rare book room at Carnegie Mellon's Hunt Hall. Later, they witnessed her in deep discussion with a group of

5

individuals outside Newell Simon, her face radiating excitement. It was evident that Aunt Loxley was pursuing something extraordinary, but the nature of her project continued to elude Attie.

Meanwhile, her mother's involvement in a groundbreaking project at a company that had built the Mars Rover Opportunity heightened her curiosity further. The company's headquarters conveniently sat in Pittsburgh's Strip neighborhood, near Carnegie Mellon University, and was a hub of technological marvels. Excited at the prospect of exploring this world, Attie decided to accompany her mom to the lab, hoping to gain some insights.

Stepping into the bustling world of scientists and engineers, the she found their conversations utterly captivating. Mentions of a program called Athenian lingered in the air, capturing their attention. Curiosity ignited as they overheard phrases like "hands-on," "curious young girls," and "incredible resume builder." Questions raced through her mind. What was Athenian? How could she become a part of it?

Driven by curiosity, Attie embarked on a journey of research, immersing herself in the world of Athenian. To her astonishment, she discovered that it drew inspiration from the Greek goddess of wisdom and courage. BeAthenian.org unveiled a breathtaking platform designed to ignite the spark of curiosity in young girls, exploring careers that had the power to move the world figuratively and literally through transportation.

With each click, her excitement grew. Athenian promised an extraordinary adventure, an immersive journey where they could get their hands dirty, learn, and make a tangible difference. It aligned perfectly with her passions and dreams, and deep inside, she knew she had to join this exclusive club.

As the possibilities unfolded, the young inventor couldn't wait to share her discoveries with Aunt Loxley. Her expertise and guidance would be invaluable on this incredible journey. Perhaps, together, they could uncover more clues behind this exciting club and find even more breathtaking opportunities.

Little did she know then, how this move to Rocket City would shape her life and set her on a path to extraordinary discoveries and adventures.

CHAPTER 2
The Freshman Glow: The First Year of High School

Back home in Huntsville, Attie eagerly embarked on her freshman year of high school. The halls were buzzing with anticipation as students reunited with old friends and forged new connections. Inspired by Taylor Swift's advice on being friends with everyone but not fitting into a clique, Attie set out to become a social butterfly, determined to make this year the best one yet.

As she navigated the bustling hallways, a glimmer of familiarity caught Attie's eye. She could have sworn she saw her adventurous Aunt Loxley disappear around a corner. Bewildered yet intrigued, Attie couldn't shake off the mysterious encounter. Aunt Loxley had always been the family's wanderlust icon, disappearing for months at a time on thrilling expeditions. Her sudden appearance only intensified the air of mystery surrounding her.

To relieve the academic stress and foster new friendships, Attie embraced her love for nature. She organized day trips to explore the breathtaking natural beauty that northern Alabama had to offer. With a group of enthusiastic classmates, she journeyed to picturesque destinations like Cane Creek Canyon, Russell Cave, and Little Natural Bridge. Surrounded by the serene landscapes, Attie not only reconnected with the wonders of nature but also forged lasting memories with her new friends, strengthening their bonds.

School life wasn't the only avenue for Attie's quest for connections. Determined to build her network and engage with new people, she decided to accompany her dad to work at Redstone Arsenal. As they made their way through security, Attie glanced out of the car window and caught sight of Aunt Loxley's distinct adventure truck passing through the guarded checkpoint. Her heart raced with excitement and curiosity. What was Aunt Loxley up to? How had she ended up here?

Unable to contain her curiosity any longer, Attie brought up her Aunt Loxley's sighting during a family dinner. However, the atmosphere in the room shifted instantly. Her parents looked at each other and a weird energy took over the room immediately. Attie knew that something was happening. And wow, Dad changed the topic so quickly he could have scored Olympian points with that maneuver!

Attie's curiosity transformed into an insatiable drive to uncover the truth. She couldn't ignore the secrets hiding within her family any longer. What had Aunt Loxley been involved in, and why were her parents so hesitant to reveal the truth? Her parents so hesitant to reveal the truth? Her freshman year took on a new dimension as she walked the halls of her high school, building new friendships and embracing the wonders of nature.

But now, Attie's journey of self-discovery was intertwined with the enigma surrounding Aunt Loxley's mysterious behavior.

With each passing day, the unanswered questions fueled her determination and propelled her into an adventure of her own. The secrets that had laid dormant for years were calling out to her, beckoning her to uncover the truth behind her aunt's mysterious ways. As she delved deeper, Attie's courage, resilience, and unwavering determination were put to the test. The answers she sought held the key to unlocking the secrets that awaited, guiding her toward a truth that went far beyond the surface.

CHAPTER 3
Where in the World is Aunt Loxley?

Attie felt a wave of frustration wash over her as she stared at her computer screen. For the past two weeks, she had been meticulously tracking Aunt Loxley's whirlwind book tour through her social media accounts. From visiting a rocket company in Huntsville to Fortune 100 companies in Atlanta, and even giving a guest lecture at Carnegie Mellon University in Pittsburgh, Aunt Loxley seemed to be everywhere at once. Attie's whiteboard resembled a chaotic mosaic, covered in a crisscross of strings that represented Aunt Loxley's numerous flights across the country.

Yet, amidst her impressive journey, Aunt Loxley had not responded to any of Attie's messages. It bothered her deeply, as their bond had always been strong. Aunt Loxley was her confidante, her guide, and her source of inspiration. The silence weighed heavily on her heart, fueling her determination to uncover the truth behind her aunt's disappearance.

However, as Attie tried to refocus her energy on school, she found herself hitting a dead end. Each passing day without any communication from Aunt Loxley left her feeling unsettled and distracted. She needed guidance, a reminder of Aunt Loxley's wise words to steer her back on track.

Attie turned to the shelves of her bookcase, lined with the works of her favorite authors. Among them stood Aunt Loxley's own published works, a testament to her creativity and brilliance. She pulled down a dog-eared copy and flipped through its pages, searching for that familiar voice of reason. Her eyes landed on a passage that seemed to have been highlighted specifically for moments like these:

"In every path we choose, there will be obstacles and uncertainties. But remember, it is during these moments of uncertainty that we are given the opportunity to truly grow. Embrace what lies ahead, for even if the road is foggy, your determination will light the way."

Attie embraced these words, knowing that they held the power to guide her past her current dilemmas. Aunt Loxley had always believed in her, instilling in her the resilience to face whatever challenges came her way. With renewed determination, she made a promise to herself to focus on her upcoming presentation and seize the opportunity that lay before her.

Yet, amid her determination to succeed academically, another concern tugged at her heartstrings. Her feelings for Tyler, her charismatic and popular teammate, had intertwined with her worries about Aunt Loxley. She believed herself to be too much of a "nerd" for someone like him to notice, fostering a sense of self-doubt that clouded her judgment. But with Aunt Loxley's words echoing in her mind, Attie knew she could not let her personal feelings derail her ambitions.

Late into the night, Attie feverishly worked on her speech, tweaking every line to captivate the minds of the judges. Every word had to convey the passion she felt for their start-up idea and showcase her ingenuity. She stood in front of her mirror, enunciating each syllable with determination and conviction. Her iPhone became her constant companion as she listened to the recording of her speech, determined to embed its essence into her subconscious.

As the days melted into one another, Attie's routine revolved around school and preparations for the upcoming junior "Shark Tank" competition. Though her concern for Aunt Loxley never waned, she channeled her energy into honing her pitch and perfecting her delivery. She believed that achieving success in this competition could potentially unlock the answers she sought and even provide a means of reconnecting with her beloved aunt.

With each passing day, Attie could feel the adrenaline building within her, ready to burst forth on the stage of the competition. The hours spent researching, refining, and rehearsing had sculpted her into a force to be reckoned with. The moment to showcase her innovative ideas and prove that dreams could become a reality was fast approaching.

CHAPTER 4
Getting Your Hands Dirty

Deep in thought, Attie found herself feeling overwhelmed and stressed. This was a familiar sensation for her, a sign that her mind was in need of a creative outlet. She had found solace in building things since she was a child, a way to escape from the chaos of everyday life and channel her emotions into something tangible.

Her current project, designing sketches for a prototype vehicle, had become an endless cycle of frustration and disappointment. Each attempt fell short of capturing the vision in her mind, leaving her feeling defeated. With a sigh, Attie decided to step away from the sketches for a moment and fix the malfunctioning vacuum cleaner that had been collecting dust in the corner of her room.

As she stared at the vacuum, a smirk crossed her face. "You would think Mom could have fixed this," she muttered under her breath, recalling her mother's prestigious title as a rocket scientist. But her mother, like many others, often got caught up in the busyness of work and overlooked the smaller domestic tasks.

Determined to take matters into her own hands, Attie gathered her tools and approached the broken vacuum cleaner. She carefully disassembled it, studying each intricate part and analyzing its functionality. Her hands moved with precision and purpose as she traced the circuitry and identified the faulty wires. With a diligent focus, she cleaned every nook and cranny, eradicating the accumulated dirt and dust.

Repairing the vacuum cleaner became a journey of discovery for Attie – a microcosm of her larger creative endeavors. It was an opportunity for her to exercise her problem-solving skills and put her knowledge to practical use. As she carefully reassembled the vacuum cleaner, piece by piece, her confidence grew with each successful step.

Finally, the moment of truth arrived. Attie took a deep breath as she plugged in the repaired vacuum cleaner. As it roared back to life, the suction stronger than ever before, a triumphant smile spread across Attie's face. She felt a rush of satisfaction knowing that she had not only fixed the problem but also reaffirmed her ability to tackle challenges head-on.

Buoyed by this surge of confidence, Attie turned her attention back to the engine she had been rebuilding as part of her personal project. There were a few more tasks to complete before she could deem it ready for sale. She reached out to Mr. Chip, her trusted mentor, and eagerly absorbed his guidance as she tightened the bolts, checked the wiring, and ensured every component was in perfect condition.

Five hours later, weary but satisfied, Attie wiped the grease off her hands and took a step back, admiring her handiwork. The engine gleamed under the workshop lights, a testament to her dedication and perseverance. With the guidance of Mr. Chip, the engine she had meticulously rebuilt was finally complete.

Now came the next phase – preparing her social media platforms and crafting captivating advertisements to announce the imminent sale of her engine. Attie knew that effectively showcasing her passion and expertise was crucial in attracting potential buyers. She meticulously curated images that showcased the engine's flawless craftsmanship, capturing its essence from various angles. Alongside the captivating visuals, she poured her heart into writing a persuasive piece that conveyed the hard work and dedication invested in the engine's reconstruction.

With a few clicks, Attie posted her engine for sale across her social media platforms. She couldn't help but feel a surge of excitement and anticipation as the comments section slowly came alive with inquiries and praise. Amidst the sea of virtual interaction, one comment caught her eye – Aunt Loxley's. Her response in their secret code was all Attie needed to know that her aunt was nearby.

To Attie, Aunt Loxley was more than just a family member. She was a mentor, confidante, and kindred spirit. Aunt Loxley, with her boisterous energy and endless tales, had always encouraged Attie's creative endeavors. They shared a unique bond, strengthened by their mutual love for storytelling and adventure.

Anticipating her aunt's arrival, Attie couldn't help but feel a sense of longing for the stories and experiences her aunt would bring from her book tour. Their shared love for exploration and discovery had fueled Attie's imagination since childhood, and she eagerly awaited the infusion of inspiration that her aunt's presence would undoubtedly bring.

As Attie sat back, basking in the satisfaction of completing her projects, she couldn't help but feel immense gratitude. The process of getting her hands dirty had not only allowed her to overcome stress and find solace but had also taught her valuable lessons in independence and self-reliance. The feeling of empowerment that stemmed from taking control and making something work had become an invaluable part of her identity.

With her engine ready for sale and Aunt Loxley on the horizon, Attie embraced the serendipity of the moment. The merging of mentorship and family offered her the guidance and support she needed to continue pursuing her dreams. It was in these moments that Attie truly felt like a budding inventor, weaving her narrative of resilience, growth, and creativity.

What projects would you like to try?

⊞ HASHTAG
yes!

My favorite songs...

CHAPTER 5
What the Code Is Going On?

Attie's parents continued to act peculiarly, leaving her feeling even more puzzled. Her dad's jumpy behavior was escalating, with him muttering "what the code" to his laptop and phone more frequently. Meanwhile, her mom seemed to be absent and away at meetings more often than usual, causing Attie to feel a bit lost and disconnected. As the hours turned into days, there was still no word from Aunt Loxley, further fueling Attie's curiosity about what was happening with all the adults in her life.

One afternoon, as Attie passed by her dad's office, she heard strange noises coming from the basement. Concerned for her safety, she quickly grabbed her phone and slipped it into her hidden pocket. She also made sure her tracker was securely attached to her, allowing her dad to effortlessly keep tabs on her whereabouts. After catching her dad's attention and gesturing towards the basement door, Attie received a nod of understanding.

Armed with a hefty flashlight, Attie cautiously descended the basement stairs, leading to her dad's studio. With a flick of a switch, the room was instantly illuminated, revealing a surprising sight. Aunt Loxley stood before her, carrying boxes and donning her usual workshop coveralls. However, she looked like an absolute mess, clearly drained from yet another one of her trademark 15-hour workdays. Attie couldn't contain her excitement and let out a joyful scream, rushing towards her aunt for a tight embrace. What initially started as a shock turned into bouts of laughter as the two of them marveled at the unexpected reunion.

Eager to help, Attie assisted Loxley in bringing in the remaining boxes and luggage. Finally settling down on the studio couch, they started swapping stories, their conversation flowing effortlessly as if no time had passed at all. Hours seemed to slip away unnoticed, and it was only when Attie noticed the first rays of the morning sun that she realized she had spent the entire night sleeping on the sofa, simply captivated by the warmth of her aunt's presence.

Climbing the stairs from the basement studio, Attie made her way to the kitchen, where a heartwarming scene awaited her. Her dad and Aunt Loxley were busy preparing breakfast together, their laughter and banter filling the room. The news they eventually shared was nothing short of extraordinary: Aunt Loxley had made the daring decision to relocate her company from the West Coast to the Southern region of Birmingham –

Atlanta - Nashville. Not only that, but she had managed to coordinate this move while on her nationwide book tour. Despite her worldly travels and recent success, Loxley had realized how much she missed the charm and deep-rooted connection she felt towards the South. While the adults exchanged knowing looks, a peculiar undercurrent of mystery seemed to linger in the air, leaving Attie struggling to comprehend the hidden depths of their shared secrets.

Filled with a mix of excitement and curiosity, Attie eagerly attended school that day. Signs seemed to continuously appear throughout her classes, further fueling her inquisitiveness. As the final bell rang, she made her way back home, determined to unravel the truth about the captivating enigma surrounding the actions of the adults in her life.

Later that evening, all four of them - Aunt Loxley, Attie's mom, dad, and Attie herself - gathered around the dinner table. The long-anticipated revelation finally emerged: Attie's mom had been selected for a groundbreaking mission to the International Space Station, and Aunt Loxley would collaborate with her from Earth. The magnitude of the news left Attie speechless, a torrent of emotions flooding her heart. There was excitement for her mom's incredible opportunity, pride in her achievements, and a tinge of worry about the risks involved.

Yet, amidst it all, Attie couldn't shake off the growing realization that her life was about to embark on an extraordinary journey of its own. With the adults keeping their secrets and venturing into uncharted territories, Attie's curiosity burned brighter than ever before. She couldn't help but wonder what incredible experiences awaited her as this new chapter of her life unfolded.

CHAPTER 6
Renaissance Woman in the Making

In her pursuit of knowledge, Attie delved deeper into the wonders of nature. She was astounded to learn that the hummingbird's ability to fly backward was not a mere coincidence but a result of its unique wing structure and wingbeat pattern. This discovery ignited her curiosity about aerodynamics and the marvels of flight. She embarked on a quest to learn more, studying the principles of lift, drag, and thrust, and even experimented with building miniature gliders to better grasp the complexities of flight.

Similarly, her fascination with dolphins and their communication system led her to explore the field of marine biology. Attie learned that each click and whistle in the dolphin's repertoire represented a specific message, allowing them to coordinate hunts, warn each other of danger, and even express emotions. The complexity of their language captivated her, inspiring a desire to understand codes and signals in all aspects of life.

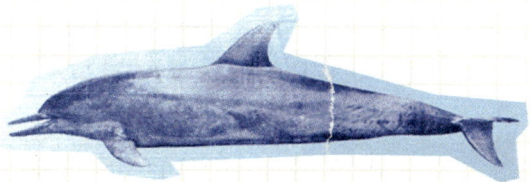

Guided by her Renaissance spirit, Attie immersed herself in the field of cryptography, marveling at the encoded messages throughout history. She uncovered the secrets of ancient civilizations, such as the hieroglyphics of Egypt and the alphabets of the Mayans, deciphering their hidden stories and intricate symbols. By studying the evolution of cryptography, Attie recognized its profound impact on communication, from wartime strategies to the modern-day encryption methods used in cybersecurity.

Her thirst for knowledge propelled Attie to explore the lives of historical figures who embodied Renaissance ideals. She admired the intellectual prowess of Leonardo da Vinci, who effortlessly transitioned between art, science, and engineering. She discovered how Da Vinci's extensive research and unique perspective as a polymath contributed to his masterpieces, such as the Mona Lisa and The Last Supper.

Attie also delved into the life of Renaissance woman Artemisia Gentileschi, an accomplished painter who defied the societal norms of her time. Inspired by Gentileschi's resilience and determination, she recognized the importance of breaking barriers and persisting in pursuing one's passions.

With every step she took, Attie reveled in the interplay between disciplines, discovering how the knowledge gained in one field could enhance and enrich her understanding of another. Each piece of information she absorbed became a brushstroke on her intellectual canvas, giving depth and dimension to her Renaissance spirit.

As a very young girl, the buildings and museums of Washington DC had been her haven. The day trips that she and her parents had taken from their home in Creativity Cove had allowed her to explore the architectural achievements that stood as testaments to human ingenuity. Attie studied the intricate designs and symbolism embedded in the city's landmarks, unraveling the hidden codes that connected the past to the present. She discovered that these structures were not just mere buildings; they were works of art, designed to communicate messages and evoke emotions.

Aunt Loxley's words resonated within Attie's soul as she ventured deeper into her journey of becoming a Renaissance woman. The signs and codes she sought were not merely external but manifestations of the knowledge she sought within herself. She realized that her quest was not solely about acquiring knowledge but about cultivating a holistic understanding of the interconnectedness of the world.

With renewed vigor, Attie embraced the Renaissance Woman mindset, ready to continue her exploration of history, art, science, and beyond. The pursuit of knowledge, creation, and self-discovery became her guiding principles as she ventured further into the endless realms of human experience. And Aunt Loxley's wisdom echoed in her mind, encouraging her to always get her hands dirty and embrace every opportunity for growth and learning.

CHAPTER 7
Loving Being a Nerd

Attie, a self-professed nerd, reveled in her unique identity and embraced it with every fiber of her being. Being a nerd was not just a label to her; it was a way of life that allowed her to constantly seek knowledge, indulge in her passions, and forge her own path. With an insatiable desire to learn, do, and experience, Attie found solace in the world of transportation, where she could immerse herself in the mechanics of different vehicles and embark on thrilling adventures.

As part of the 5% of kinesthetic learners, Attie understood that traditional learning methods could only take her so far. She reveled in the opportunity to get her hands dirty and learn through tangible experiences. Textbooks and lectures alone couldn't satisfy her thirst for knowledge; she needed to touch, feel, and interact with the physical world to truly understand and appreciate it.

Driving became one of Attie's greatest passions, as she relished the exhilaration of being in control of a powerful machine. Through her tireless efforts, she mastered the intricacies of each vehicle's system, understanding how gears shifted, brakes engaged, and engines roared. From sleek sports cars that hugged the road to rugged off-road vehicles that conquered the toughest terrain, Attie relished the distinct characteristics and capabilities of each automobile.

However, Attie's love for transportation extended far beyond the freedom of the open road. She craved the sensation of soaring through the sky, and flying became an integral part of her identity. She dedicated herself to learning the skills necessary to pilot various aircraft, from small gliders and propeller planes to jets and helicopters. The feeling of weightlessness and the awe-inspiring views from above captivated her. As she looked down upon the world from her cockpit, Addie marveled at the beauty of the clouds, the majesty of mountains, and the glittering lights of cities below.

But Attie's journey didn't stop at land and sky. She yearned for maritime adventures, intrigued by the vastness and mystery of the ocean. Taking on the role of "Captain Attie," she delved into the world of sailing boats, yachts, and massive cruise ships. Navigating the ebb and flow of the waves, she learned to read the wind, chart her course, and steer through uncharted waters. The vastness of the ocean became her ally, opening doors to unexplored territories and inviting her to embrace the unknown.

Being a nerd had far-reaching implications for Attie; it was a lifestyle that extended beyond her love for transportation. Her thirst for knowledge was insatiable, leading her down a myriad of diverse paths. Delving into subjects such as astronomy, art history, quantum physics, and literature, Attie expanded her understanding of the world and nurtured her intellectual curiosity. Being a nerd, to her, meant never settling for complacency and always embracing new challenges.

Her natural talent for driving and piloting every mode of transportation that she could find kept drawing her back to the club that she had found online. She really needed to dig deeper into Athenian and convince her parents to let her get involved. Attie's devotion to the Athenian Creed further strengthened her identity as a nerd. She courageously chose the path of growth, even when it seemed daunting and filled with uncertainty. Confronting her fears head-on, she understood that true growth resided on the other side of her comfort zone. Attie's character blossomed as she conducted herself with integrity and kindness, always prioritizing honesty, dependability, and selflessness. By bettering herself and her team, she embodied the essence of the creed and left a lasting impact.

Confidence became Attie's greatest ally in her nerdy endeavors. She recognized that true confidence was a result of continuously honing her skills and striving to become a better person. By embracing her abilities, maintaining her unique perspective, and valuing her sufficiency, she became her own cheerleader in any situation. Attie understood that her self-assurance was not rooted in external validation but in her unwavering belief in herself and her dreams.

As Attie continued her nerdy pursuits, her love for being a nerd only grew stronger. It was more than just a label; it was a journey of self-discovery, growth, and boundless exploration. Each day brought new opportunities for her to immerse herself in the wonders of the world and the pursuit of knowledge. With each endeavor, Attie wholeheartedly embraced her inner nerd, reveling in the joy of learning, doing, and experiencing the extraordinary.

5%

I love being me because:

CHAPTER 8
Presenting Like It's Shark Tank

Deep within Attie's business brain, the dream of joining the three-comma club burned brightly. It wasn't about the accumulation of wealth for her; it was about the power to make a meaningful impact on the world. She yearned to build and create, to bring forth ideas that could positively shape the future. This was her purpose, her driving force.

With this mindset, Attie approached her presentation as though she were stepping onto the grand stage of "Shark Tank" ready to pitch her groundbreaking idea to none other than the famed entrepreneur and billionaire, Mark Cuban. She had studied countless episodes, meticulously observing how successful entrepreneurs captured the judges' attention and secured investments. Attie knew that in order to stand out among the crowd, she needed to exude unwavering confidence and contagious passion.

However, there was one thing that threatened to consume her thoughts and sabotage her focus: her secret crush on her teammate, Tyler. It was a feeling she had buried deep within, hesitant to let it distract her from her goals. As she prepared herself for the monumental moment at school, Attie made a pact with herself. No matter how shaken she might feel by her emotions, she would not let them overshadow her performance. This was her chance to prove herself and to be recognized for her merit and talent.

But just as Attie was about to step on the stage, her heart filled with a mix of excitement and anxiety, she received disheartening news from her drama teacher. Tyler, her partner in this endeavor, had fallen severely ill, his voice stolen by a merciless bout of laryngitis and the flu. Attie's heart sank, and her dreams of presenting as a dynamic duo shattered. She had envisioned their synergy and camaraderie intensifying their pitch, drawing the judges in with their exceptional teamwork. Now, her solo performance would determine the fate of their concept.

The weight of this unexpected burden pressed upon Attie's shoulders, threatening to crush her spirit. Doubts crept in, whispering cruel questions about her ability to hold the audience's attention without Tyler by her side. Yet, deep inside, Attie knew she had to summon the strength to rise above her disappointment. She had prepared diligently and believed in the potential of their idea. She visualized the   judges, including the enigmatic secret judge whom she had heard in the past hour ask thought-provoking questions during other's presentations. Being able to watch the other students present and listen to the judges ask questions had struck a chord within Attie, igniting a fire within her to articulate their creation more eloquently and compellingly.

As Attie took the stage, a transformation swept over her. In that moment, she channeled the energy of the great minds who had stood before her - the inventors, the dreamers, and the game-changers. In her mind's eye, she saw Elon Musk, Marie Curie, and Da Vinci, each leaving an indelible mark on history through their perseverance and unwavering passion. She found solace in their audacity, drawing strength from their unwavering determination.

With each word she spoke, every gesture she made, Attie's passion radiated through her being. She took the audience on a journey, captivating them with the story behind their idea and showcasing the working prototype with finesse. Her movements were fluid and filled with purpose, demonstrating her deep understanding of the concept. The audience listened with rapt attention, their eyes fixed upon Attie as if hypnotized by her animated presentation and the unwavering conviction in her voice.

Finally, the moment arrived when Attie responded to the final question from the judges. It was during this interactive exchange that she felt a particular connection with the question posed by the secret judge. It was constructed with care and precision, delving into the core essence of their creation. The question resonated with her, tapping into a spark within her that propelled her to explain their idea with even greater depth and clarity. The voice behind it sounded hauntingly familiar, awakening her curiosity and leaving her eager to uncover the true identity of the mysterious figure who had shaped her moment of triumph.

As the room erupted into thunderous applause at the end of her dynamic presentation, Attie savored the electrifying wave of exhilaration that surged through her. She knew she had given her all, leaving no room for doubts or regrets. The pride in her accomplishment mingled with a burning desire to discover the true identity of the secret judge – the individual who had played a pivotal role in her moment of triumph. Little did Attie know that this encounter would set her on a path she never could have foreseen, launching her into a new and exhilarating chapter of her amazing adventures.

With every step she took away from that stage, she could feel a profound shift within herself. The mark of this presentation would forever be etched in her memory as the turning point where she proved her worth and unveiled her potential to the world. It was a validation of her dreams and aspirations, propelling her towards even greater triumphs yet to come. And among those triumphs, the revelation of the secret judge's identity would play a pivotal role, shaping her future in ways she could never have imagined.

CHAPTER 9
The Surprise Keynote Speaker

As all of the presentations came to an end, the auditorium buzzed with anticipation. Attie's heart raced as the keynote speaker was introduced. She couldn't believe her eyes. Aunt Loxley?! Her jaw dropped, and she turned to Jenny, who mirrored her disbelief. How could Aunt Loxley be the speaker? And what was this about a special announcement being the framework for her speech?

As Aunt Loxley took the stage, a wave of inspiration washed over the room. She captivated the audience with her powerful words, sharing personal stories of her dreams, challenges, and triumphs. She spoke about the importance of pursuing passions fearlessly and embracing failures as part of the journey towards success.

Attie couldn't help but be swept away by Aunt Loxley's words. It was as if the universe had orchestrated this moment, bringing all the dots of her journey together. But nothing could have prepared her for what came next.

Aunt Loxley's gaze shifted towards Attie and Jenny, eyes sparkling with mischief. She took a deep breath and made the announcement that left the entire auditorium in awe.

43

"My young friends, I have something extraordinary to share with you all tonight. The company I recently moved to the Birmingham-Atlanta-Nashville region is none other than Athenian—the exact club that Attie has been talking about to all of you, the club she yearns to join."

Gasps filled the room as questions raced through Attie's mind. How did Aunt Loxley create the perfect club for her to join without her knowing? Was it mere coincidence, or was something more profound at play? Attie felt a mix of excitement and urgency. She knew she needed to ask Aunt Loxley all these burning questions tonight at dinner.

But before Attie could fully process the astonishing revelation, it was time to announce the winner of the presentation competition. Aunt Loxley held her breath, her nerves intertwining with those of the participants as she reached into the envelope. The room fell silent, anticipation thick in the air.

A smile graced Aunt Loxley's face as she called Jenny, Attie's BFF, to the stage. The cheers erupted throughout the auditorium as it was announced that Jenny's concept of an Ai app that streamlined project management had amassed the winning amount of points.

The excitement grew as Aunt Loxley continued, revealing that the judges were equally impressed by Attie's transportation concept, voting it as their favorite for the "Shoot for the Moon" award.

Attie and Jenny's eyes met, brimming with unfiltered joy and astonishment. They squealed and embraced each other tightly, their dreams intertwining with the recognition they had received. It was a moment they would forever cherish, a testament to their hard work and the support they had given each other.

With the competition concluded, it was time to celebrate. Attie and Jenny dashed out of the auditorium, their laughter filling the hallway as they headed to get a snack at their favorite bakery. The tingling in their stomachs lingered, a sweet mix of victory and anticipation for the evening conversation with Aunt Loxley that lay ahead.

As they settled into a cozy corner of the shop, Attie couldn't help but rattle off the thoughts that raced through her mind. How did Aunt Loxley create Athenian? Was it all a coincidence or part of a grand plan? She yearned to uncover the truth, to understand the depths of this inexplicable connection.

Jenny leaned in, her eyes filled with curiosity. "Attie, what if Aunt Loxley has been silently guiding us towards our dreams all along? What if she saw the spark within you and created Athenian to help you thrive?"

Attie's eyes widened, realization dawning upon her. "That's it, Jenny! It all makes sense now. Aunt Loxley has been planting seeds of inspiration, shaping our paths without us even realizing it. I can't wait to hear what she has to say over dinner tonight. There's a whole world of possibilities waiting to be unveiled."

Their conversation grew deeper, thoughts intertwining as they savored their treats and nurtured their dreams. The bakery became a sanctuary of anticipation and wonder, a place where dreams melded with reality. As they prepared to meet Aunt Loxley for dinner, Attie and Jenny knew that this evening would not only unravel the mysteries that surrounded Athenian but also set their lives on a course filled with adventure and possibility.

CHAPTER 10
The Changes Keep Coming!

Back at home after school, Attie walked through the front door with a mix of curiosity and frustration. As she descended the staircase, she could hear the faint sound of activity coming from the studio. Without hesitation, Attie pushed the door open, ready to demand answers.

"Okay, what gives?!?" Attie exclaimed, her frustration evident in her tone. "Were you ever planning on updating me on EVERYTHING that you have been doing?" She stood in the doorway, her arms crossed defiantly.

Aunt Loxley turned towards Attie with a gentle smile and motioned for her to come in. "Sit down, my little inventor," she said, patting the cushioned chair next to her. "There's so much I want to tell you, and I apologize for not filling you in sooner. I've been so caught up in this new project that I neglected to keep you in the loop. But now that you're here, let me tell you all about it."

As Attie settled into the chair, Aunt Loxley began to unravel the story behind Athenian, recounting not just its creation but the very essence of why she started it. She spoke of the undeniable spark of excitement she saw in Attie's eyes when she assigned her those early projects during her childhood. It was in those moments that Aunt Loxley realized the immense passion and potential not just in Attie, but in all young girls who dared to dream big.

"I knew then, my dear, that there was something special in you," Aunt Loxley's voice was filled with emotion as she spoke. "And I wanted to create a space where girls like us could thrive, where we could break free from societal expectations and explore the full extent of our potential."

She paused for a moment, reflecting on their shared history. "I realized that there are so many amazing opportunities for girls in STREAM careers, especially those related to transportation. I wanted to create a space where girls who are passionate about improving the world through innovation and making things move could come together and learn from each other."

She explained how, in those early days, she had meticulously planned and strategized the founding of Athenian. Every detail was carefully considered, from the curriculum to the outreach programs.

Aunt Loxley poured her heart and soul into every aspect of the organization, fueled by her unwavering belief in empowering girls in

STREAM-related careers, especially those tied to transportation.

Addie's annoyance started to fade away, replaced by a glimmer of excitement. "So, you started a club for girls like us?" she asked, her eyes lighting up with anticipation.

Loxley smiled warmly and nodded. "I did. I started Athenian, a nonprofit organization dedicated to empowering girls and showing them a variety of career opportunities... like designing car interiors or engineering a special component on a rocket. But just as I was getting things off the ground, COVID hit. The world went into lockdown, and we were all confined to our homes." Attie's eyebrows raise in surprise. Had Aunt Loxley been through so much without her even realizing?

"It was a tumultuous time, Attie," Loxley continued, her voice tinged with a mix of pride and resilience. "In California, we were stuck indoors for months. Our lives turned upside down, and even going for a walk on the beach could result in police-issued tickets. The whole world seemed to come to a standstill. It was disheartening, but at that moment, I made a decision."

Attie leaned in closer, captivated by her aunt's words. "What did you decide, Aunt Loxley?!?"

Loxley's eyes brighten as she recounts her journey. "Instead of giving up like many others, I chose to devote myself 24/7 to building Athenian. I knew the immense potential it held, and I refused to let the circumstances stop me. Even when the rich individuals, foundations, and corporations halted their giving and refused to provide funding to a brand-new nonprofit, I never stopped. I was fueled by sheer determination."

Attie's admiration for her aunt deepened with every word. She had always known Loxley to be resilient, but this was another level.

"I believed in the mission so strongly that I knew I had to keep going, no matter what," Loxley says passionately. "I collaborated with brilliant minds virtually, held online workshops, and connected with girls from all over the world who shared our vision. It was a challenging time, but it also allowed us to adapt and innovate. We couldn't let a lockdown silence our dreams."

It was during a well-deserved holiday break that Aunt Loxley found herself reflecting on her journey, feeling the weight of her experiences and the lessons she had learned. And in a moment of clarity, she knew that her story needed to be shared. Attie's eyes sparkle with admiration and inspiration as she looks at her aunt. "And now you've written a book? That's amazing!"

The book tour that followed was an eye-opening experience. Loxley met countless individuals who, inspired by her story, began to believe in their dreams once again. But it was during these encounters that Aunt Loxley made a profound decision. She realized that the impact she desired to make through Athenian could flourish best in a community steeped in innovation, invention, and historical significance.

And so, Aunt Loxley chose to move Athenian back to the South, her beloved home. The South held deep meaning and connections for her, with a rich history of inventors and innovators who had shaped the world. Aunt Loxley believed that this setting would not only provide the nurturing environment Athenian needed to grow but would also serve as a launching pad for a new generation of talented minds.

As Aunt Loxley concluded her tale, a profound silence filled the room. Attie absorbed every word, a newfound respect and admiration blooming within her. Aunt Loxley's journey had been one of immense determination, facing countless setbacks and struggles with unwavering strength. She had never backed down in her belief in the power of young girls to shape the world.

Tough situations I've handled gracefully...

CHAPTER 11
The Dinner of Celebration

That night over dinner, the four of them basked in the joy of Attie's successful presentation. The table was filled with laughter and heartfelt congratulations as they celebrated her being awarded the Judge's "Shoot for the Moon" Award. Attie's parents beamed with pride, knowing that their daughter had captivated the audience with her innovative concept.

Aunt Loxley, always the wise observer, chimed in with her unique perspective. "You know," she began, her eyes sparkling with wisdom, "sometimes it's better to win the award that draws attention, rather than the biggest one with the prize. By winning the Judge's Moonshot Award, you've not only amazed everyone with your concept but also created a lasting impression. Companies, universities, and future employers will be intrigued by your originality and creativity."

Attie's heart swelled with gratitude for her aunt's encouragement. She understood the value of this recognition and how it could open doors to endless opportunities.

As the conversation flowed, the atmosphere took a bittersweet turn. Mom gathered the family's attention, her voice filled with mixed emotions. "I have an update on my mission to the

55

International Space Station," she announced, her eyes shining with excitement and a tinge of sadness. "The launch date is becoming more defined, and I will be leaving for at least six months. The planning and preparations for the project are going to consume all of my time as I prepare."

A wave of emotions washed over Attie. She had always admired her mother's brilliance and passion for exploration, but now the reality of her absence was hitting home.

Aunt Loxley, who had been quietly observing, caught Attie's eye and exchanged a knowing look, as if to say, "We've got this."

Attie took a deep breath, mustering the courage to reassure her mother. "You don't have to worry about me, Mom. Aunt Loxley is here with me, and we're going to make Athenian thrive together. You go out there and show the world how brilliant you are. I can't wait to talk to you from Earth while you're up in space, sharing stories of our triumphs and adventures."

Mom's face softened, filled with a mix of pride and gratitude. She nodded, knowing in her heart that Attie had inherited her determination and resilience. She had raised a daughter who could conquer any challenge, no matter the distance that separated them.

Fearless ♡

CHAPTER 12
When Fame Comes Knocking

The next morning, an excited squeal echoed throughout the house, jolting Attie awake from her peaceful slumber. She blinked her sleep-filled eyes and listened intently as Aunt Loxley's footsteps raced toward her room. Before Attie could fully comprehend what was happening, her aunt burst into the room, a wide grin plastered across her face.

"Attie, this is what I was talking about!" Aunt Loxley exclaimed, waving her phone in the air. "Here is why I say it sometimes works out better NOT to win the top award!"

Attie, still groggy and confused, rubbed the sleep out of her eyes and glanced at the glowing screen. Her jaw dropped in disbelief. "What?! A million-plus views about me? What is this?" Her eyes widened as she perused Jenny's YouTube channel, their go-to outlet for posting silly videos – often featuring Attie inventing things, occasionally blowing them up, and then fixing them while discussing the lessons learned from each failure. On the channel, Jenny shared her expertise in coding, computers, and making difficult concepts appear easy-breezy for all the "dummies".

"Congratulations to both of my Swifties," a comment read, Taylor Swift's name clearly visible beneath it. Attie's heart raced with excitement. THE Taylor Swift had seen and commented on this viral video that Jenny had posted! OMG!!!

School that day was an absolute blast. The entire student body was abuzz with celebration, marveling at what Attie and Jenny had achieved together, even as competitors. Sure, Jenny had won the competition, earning the coveted summer internship that everyone dreamed of. However, Attie and Jenny had managed to bring forth a fervor surrounding what their teenage spirit, determination, and teamwork could accomplish.

As if the excitement at school wasn't enough, Attie's phone suddenly erupted with a flurry of notifications. Emails, texts, and DMs poured in from businesses and people all around the world. Attie's head spun with exhilaration as she juggled responding to messages from potential collaborators and internships from far-flung places.

It was as if fame had come knocking on Attie's door, and she couldn't quite believe it. The promise of new opportunities shimmered before her, and she began to comprehend the immense impact they had made with their video. It wasn't just about inning competitions or gaining individual recognition. It was about showing the world that teenage girls could excel, inspire, and celebrate each other's accomplishments.

Through the whirlwind of attention, Attie realized that this newfound fame came with responsibilities. She understood that she had the power to motivate young minds and encourage them to pursue their passions fearlessly. Her imagination, combined with Jenny's technical wizardry and the unbreakable bond they shared, had resonated with countless individuals.

With each response she typed, Attie's words took on a conversational tone, filled with genuine excitement and encouragement. She realized that her journey had just begun, and there was so much more to explore, create, and innovate.

As she delved deeper into the world of science, technology, research, engineering, arts, and mathematics (STREAM), Attie discovered a vast network of like-minded individuals and organizations eager to join forces. She engaged in conversations with tech companies, universities, and advocacy groups, discussing potential collaborations and initiatives to empower more girls in STREAM fields. Attie's passion for writing and storytelling also found its place in her newfound fame. She began documenting her experiences, crafting inspiring narratives that spoke to the struggles and triumphs of being a female innovator in a traditionally male-dominated industry. She aimed to share her journey, not just with those who idolized her, but with anyone who dared to dream beyond societal limitations.

be
happy ♡

DReAM
Big

Awesome!

GOOD
ENERGY

Yes
you
can

"One
of a
kind"

You've
Got the
POWER

You"
Got
This!

Brave
be

CHAPTER 13
Athenian Comes to Town

Jennie and Attie were deep in conversation as they walked down the hall. When suddenly they bumped into Aunt Loxley and Attie's favorite teacher, Dr. Borne.

"Just the person we wanted to see!" Loxley exclaimed. "Dr. Borne and I were just discussing what your next steps should be. We're talking about starting a special concentration within Athenian and developing divisions of Athenian clubs based in cities across the USA so that you and your friends can meet locally in-person to discuss ideas and support each other. The librarian at your school just said that she wants to spearhead this idea with you for all of the girls based in Huntsville. All of you being able to support each other just like you and Jenny did yesterday. I mean, a million views on a viral video overnight. That type of magic needs to be shared and amplified with your friends. Like-minds make the magic happen, you know."

The idea of a special concentration within Athenian intrigued Attie. It meant diving deeper into her passions and exploring subjects she truly loved.

The prospect of learning alongside like-minded peers excited her, knowing they could collaborate and push each other to reach new heights. She imagined the interesting discussions and projects they could embark on together, expanding their understanding and knowledge.

Dr. Borne and Loxley spent the rest of the afternoon with Attie and Jenny, delving into the details of their plans. They discussed the importance of incorporating internships into the program. Dr. Borne explained that internships were not only valuable for gaining practical experience but also for developing essential skills and building professional networks. Attie's eyes widened as she envisioned herself working alongside professionals in her field of interest, learning from their expertise and forming connections that could potentially become lifelong mentors.

They all discussed how to improve upon what Aunt Loxley had created. How to get this out to more girls who want to move the world and have fun learning how to do it?

As they were jumping around through pages on the website, Attie wrote down the pieces that stood out to her.

The core values summed it up best:
Character, Courage, Confidence and Commitment.

And the Manifesto was Attie's favorite:

"Athenians strive to become the best version of themselves. They are willing to challenge themselves, take risks, and try new things. Athenians take initiative and work hard to finish their commitments. These girls are preparing to become successful by learning various life skills that aren't taught in school. Athenians aren't just dreamers, they are the leaders of the future."

With these values ingrained in her mind, Attie couldn't help but feel a sense of awe and inspiration as she read over The Athenians' Manifesto. It resonated deeply with her, and she could see how these values encompassed everything that Aunt Loxley had stood for throughout her career and life. The Manifesto was a guide to becoming the best version of oneself and preparing for a successful future, just as Aunt Loxley had done.

Aunt Loxley's belief in Attie's abilities was evident when she asked if she was ready to take on a leadership role in Athenian. It was a moment that both excited and intimidated Attie. She had always looked up to Aunt Loxley, admired her accomplishments, and wanted to follow in her footsteps. Now, she had the chance to make a real impact and help grow the business that Aunt Loxley had dedicated her life to.

With a surge of determination, Attie accepted the challenge. She recognized this as an opportunity not only to contribute to Athenian but also to learn about entrepreneurship herself. The thought of stepping into a leadership role and guiding other girls on their journeys filled her with a mix of excitement and nerves. But deep down, she knew she was ready for this responsibility.

CHAPTER 14
What Happens Next?

Attie's days in Athenian were busy yet fulfilling. Her viral video and the connections she had made were just the special sauce on a spectacular couple of days.

Now it was time for her to get serious with her intentions and start planning for an internship in six months. A lot to do for the new girl in town!

As Attie dove headfirst into her preparations, she soon realized that there was even more to be done before she could fully embrace her role as a leader in Athenian. The enthusiasm and support she had received from the community were heartwarming, but she knew she needed to earn their trust and respect through tangible actions.

What would the future hold for her? Would her dreams come true, or would she face disappointment and setbacks? Only time will tell. But one thing was certain – Attie was determined to carve her path and make a difference in the world. With her passion, creativity, and unyielding spirit, there was no limit to what she could achieve. That night, as the family gathered in the living room to bask in the heat from the fireplace, there was an air of celebration and anticipation. Aunt Loxley's decision to move to the same city as Attie's family and join them under the same roof brought joy to everyone. It was a chance for family bonds to grow stronger and for Attie to have her beloved aunt close by, providing support and inspiration.

But the excitement didn't stop there. Attie's mom had received an incredible opportunity to go up to the International Space Station. Her project on gardening in space caught the attention of NASA, and she was selected to contribute her expertise to the groundbreaking research. The family marveled at the magnitude of the achievement, knowing that her work would have a lasting impact on space exploration and colonization.

Of course, Attie couldn't forget her accomplishments being chosen for the Judge's "Shoot for the Moon" award for her transportation concept. Jenny's video of her had gone viral and accumulated a million views overnight. The recognition and positive feedback filled her with a sense of pride. But what truly touched her heart was having a best friend like Jenny who always had her back, even in the face of competition. The bond they shared was unbreakable, and Attie was grateful for the support and friendship they had built over the months.

As the family reveled in their individual successes, there was one person who stood out with an extra sparkle in his eye - Attie's father. He seemed exceptionally happy, hinting at a secret that he couldn't expand on. Curiosity sparked within Attie as she observed her dad's excitement.

It was time to tickle some answers out of him and unravel the mystery behind that twinkle in his eye.

Little did Attie know that this chapter of her life was about to take an unexpected turn, leading her on a new adventure filled with surprises, growth, and endless possibilities. Where would her adventure go next?

She's the real deal (and a real person). Meet my Aunt Loxley...

Loxley Browne

Let's get something straight: Loxley Browne wasn't born with a silver spoon in her mouth or a perfect plan for world domination. Nope. She was born with muddy boots on her feet and a suitcase in her hand, figuratively and literally. You see, Loxley wasn't just a farm girl. She wasn't just a city girl. She was both.

Cue the split-screen life.

The child of divorced parents (yeah, that club is bigger than you think), Loxley grew up toggling between two totally different worlds. On one side, the farm: dirt roads, horse stalls, the smell of fresh-cut hay, and sunrises that made you feel like the sky was showing off just for you. On the other side, the city: concrete, coffee shops, so many people, and big ideas floating through skyscraper reflections. Two homes. Two versions of normal. And from the outside? It might have looked complicated. But for Loxley, it was magic.

71

On the farm, she wasn't afraid to get her hands dirty... literally. She wrangled horses like a cowgirl, drove a tractor before she could properly reach the pedals, raised bees (yep, real live buzzing ones), and repaired fences with nothing but wire, willpower, and a hammer she found in the barn dust. Nature was her mentor. It taught her the value of patience, the beauty of quiet, and the fact that the best kind of strength often comes without applause. Grit, resilience, and creativity weren't just personality traits, they were survival tools.

After flying through Brownies and Girl Scouts (she won first prize for a chocolate cake, by the way), Loxley needed something more. Enter: 4-H, a youth leadership and learning club that became HER place. She dove in headfirst. Demonstrations, entomology (yep, bug science), public speaking, community leadership, she did it all.

She even went to Nationals in entomology and mastered. Not kidding. While other kids were screaming over weird bugs, Loxley was out there with her bug jars, magnifying glass, and a brain full of Latin insect names.

And summer camp? Forget glamping. 4-H camp was real-life adventure. Campfires, archery, independence, and new friends... it was pure joy. If you ever get the chance to go to a sleepaway camp, Loxley insists you go. She'll even help you pack.

When Loxley hit her teens, life was basically:

gymnastics, manage a 21-herd horse farm (yes, really), race between after-school clubs like yearbook, drama, cheerleading, and numerous meetings, while still keep her grades high.

She loved vocational classes like drafting (where she sketched out blueprints for fun), adored history, and was obsessed with telling stories through photography.

Her biggest inspiration? Steve McCurry's green-eyed girl on the cover of "National Geographic." That image planted a seed that would grow into Loxley's lifelong passion: capturing emotion and truth in a single shot.

Then came the city.

The city taught her how to read a room, spot a fake, and blend in without disappearing. It gave her culture and confidence. It sharpened her edges and widened her lens. Gone was the purely naive, wide-eyed country girl. In her place grew someone elegant, clever, street-smart, and let's be honest, just a little bit regal.

Loxley could hang with the cowboys and the creatives, fix a broken water pump and pitch an idea in a boardroom. She wasn't one thing or the other. She was both. And more.

When she was 12, she made a decision: "I'm going to design everything." She wasn't kidding. Homes, furniture, gardens, vehicles, even consumer products. If it could be built or reimagined, Loxley wanted in.

She chased that dream into college, earning a degree in design and later another in education. The early '90s recession may have slowed her path, but she just pivoted. Reinvention was part of her DNA.

Then, just when you thought she couldn't get cooler, Loxley started racing cars. Autocrossing with the Sports Car Club of America, she drove a special 10th Anniversary 1988 RX-7 twin turbo and came in 1/10 of a second behind the national champ. She was fearless behind the wheel, constantly challenging herself to improve.

Because that's the thing about Loxley: she never stops learning, never stops growing.

Learning to live between two worlds gave her what she now calls her "superpower." It's the kind of thing that doesn't come with a cape or theme music, but it's way cooler. She could walk into any room – barn, boardroom, art studio, school auditorium – and belong. Why? Because she knew how to listen. How to observe. How to show up as herself, even when "herself" was made up of a million different pieces.

And while she was building this unstoppable version of herself, she also built something else: her pack.

Her pack wasn't chosen by blood, but by bond. They were the friends who became family. The people who showed up when life got messy, who shared snacks and secrets, who hyped each other up like unpaid motivational speakers. They were her safe space and her launch pad. They reminded her, on the hard days, that she didn't have to do everything alone. (Newsflash: No one does.)

That pack? That tribe? They shaped her. They taught her about loyalty, about laughter that fixes everything, and about how love – the fierce, platonic, ride-or-die kind – can carry you across any canyon.

So here's the truth you might need to hear right now:

If you ever feel torn between two worlds...
If you feel like you're made of mismatched parts...
If you're still figuring out who you are and how to walk in that truth...

You're not broken.
You're becoming.

You're becoming someone layered, powerful, and fully your own.

Just like Loxley did.

And who knows? Maybe your story is still about muddy boots and sharp city lights right now. Maybe it's awkward friendships, brave experiments, and embarrassing outfits from three years ago (RIP to those middle school fashion choices). But it's yours. And if you keep showing up, keep learning, and keep growing?

You're going to be unstoppable, too.

Just like Loxley Browne.

Hey there, fellow doodler, dreamer, and future inventor!

I know you like to scribble in the margins. Me too. That's exactly why I made this book the way I did.

When I was younger, my favorite books were the ones I would write in. I'd underline important words, sketch wild ideas, and jot down whatever I was feeling or building in my head. So I thought... why not create a book that actually invites you to do the same?

Think of your Charms book as part story, part secret lab notebook. Use the graph paper to dream big. Want to invent something? Sketch it. Have a thought that just has to be written down? Go for it. Need to plan your own mission, write out your goals, or doodle your future? These pages are yours.

This is more than a book, it's your personal dreamer's journal. So read, explore, and doodle away! I created this just for you.

Have fun with it,
Aunt L♥xley

Ways that I am unstoppable:

Skills that I want to learn:

Great things that I have done:

Places I would like to go:

People I admire:
(and would like to learn from)

Welcome to the Secret Book Society

(Not-so-secret if you're reading this... but still very cool.)

If you're reading Charms, then you're already one of us: a reader, a fan, a doer — a real-life dreamer ready to level up your charming skills and craft a high school resume that stands out like a jetpack at a science fair.

The Secret Book Society is your all-access pass to behind-the-scenes magic, creative adventures, and real-world skills that help you become the hero of your own story.

Here's what you get when you join:

- Monthly Newsletter — Packed with inspiration, updates, and missions.

- Exclusive Downloads — Tools, blueprints, and secret clues you won't find anywhere else.

- Video Messages from Aunt Loxley — Because she always knows what to say.

- Virtual Plot Twist Meetings — Help shape the next adventure in the Charms universe!

Yep, you read that right – you're not just reading the story, you're in it. Secret Book Society members get to weigh in on characters, help decide what happens next, and connect the dots between fiction and real life.

Think of it like the Secret Service of storytelling: you're out there making things happen, guiding the mission, helping others, and no one even knows the full power you have. Together, we make the world (and the story) better. So what are you waiting for?

Unlock your membership at BeAthenian.org and join the society. We've been expecting you.

Important ideas that I want to discuss at the next Secret Book Society ...

Downloads = Extra Charm Power

Each Charms book comes with a secret stash of downloadable goodies waiting for you online. These aren't just extras, they're tools to help you try out the same skills Attie is learning in her adventures. From invention blueprints to journaling prompts, design challenges to secret codes, every download is part of your own journey to becoming a next-level creator.

Sometimes it's something fun (hello, custom Charms-style Valentine's cards 💌).

Other times, it's the start of a full-on project with layers you can unlock as you go.

Kind of like a mystery, a mission, and a maker kit all rolled into one.

Head to BeAthenian.org to see what's available for your book, and keep checking back. You never know what Attie's up to next... and what she might share with you.

Ready to level up your charm game? Let's go!

Have you downloaded this month's project and taken action?

☐ Yes! Loving it – big things are happening!

☐ Ugh, buried in schoolwork – no time to escape!

☐ Nope... just here, letting my brain collect dust.

I want to BE...

- ☐ inventor
- ☐ builder
- ☐ engineer
- ☐ designer
- ☐ communicator
- ☐ CHARMing
- ☐

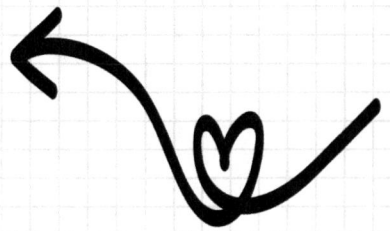